The Velveteen Rabbit and Other Animal Adventures

Selected and edited by
Nichola Trayler-Barbrook

with illustrations by
Claire Ruddock

WORDSWORTH CLASSICS

For my husband
ANTHONY JOHN RANSON
with love from your wife, the publisher.
Eternally grateful for your unconditional love.

Readers who are interested in other titles from
Wordsworth Editions are invited to visit our website at
www.wordsworth-editions.com

For our latest list and a full mail-order service, contact
Bibliophile Books, 5 Datapoint, South Crescent, London E16 4TL
TEL: +44 (0)20 7474 2474 FAX: +44 (0)20 7474 8589
ORDERS: orders@bibliophilebooks.com
WEBSITE: www.bibliophilebooks.com

First published in 2015 by Wordsworth Editions Limited
8B East Street, Ware, Hertfordshire SG12 9HJ

ISBN 978 1 84022 578 5

Text copyright © Wordsworth Editions Limited 2015
Illustrations copyright © Claire Ruddock 2015

Wordsworth® is a registered trademark of
Wordsworth Editions Limited

Wordsworth Editions
is the company founded in 1987 by
MICHAEL TRAYLER

Typeset in Great Britain by Antony Gray
Printed and bound by Clays Ltd, St Ives plc

THE
VELVETEEN
RABBIT

THERE
WAS ONCE A

velveteen rabbit, and in the beginning he was really splendid. He was fat and bunchy, as a rabbit should be; his coat was spotted brown and white, he had real thread whiskers, and his ears were lined with pink sateen. On Christmas morning, when he sat wedged in the top of the Boy's stocking, with a sprig of holly between his paws, the effect was charming.

There were other things in the stocking – nuts and oranges and a toy engine, and chocolate almonds and a clockwork mouse – but the Rabbit was quite the best of all. For at least two hours the Boy loved him, and then aunts and uncles came to dinner, and there was a great rustling of tissue paper and unwrapping of parcels, and in the excitement of looking at all the new presents the Velveteen Rabbit was forgotten.

For a long time he lived in the toy cupboard or on the nursery floor, and no one thought very much about him. He was naturally shy, and being only made of velveteen, some of the more expensive toys quite snubbed him. The mechanical toys were very superior, and looked down upon everyone else; they were full

of modern ideas, and pretended they were real. The model boat, who had lived through two seasons and lost most of his paint, caught the tone from them and

never missed an opportunity of referring to his rigging in technical terms. The Rabbit could not claim to be a model of anything, for he didn't know that real rabbits existed: he thought they were all stuffed with sawdust like himself, and he understood that sawdust was quite out of date and should never be mentioned in modern circles. Even Timothy, the jointed wooden lion, who was made by the disabled soldiers and should have had broader views, put on airs and pretended he was connected with Government. Between them all the poor little Rabbit was made to feel himself very insignificant and commonplace, and the only person who was kind to him at all was the Skin Horse.

The Skin Horse had lived longer in the nursery than any of the others. He was so old that his brown coat was bald in patches and showed the seams under-neath, and most of the hairs in his tail had been pulled out to string bead necklaces. He was wise, for he had seen a long succession of mechanical toys arrive to boast and swagger, and by and by break their mainsprings and pass away, and he knew that they were only toys, and would never turn into anything else. For nursery magic is very strange and wonderful, and only those playthings that are old and wise and experienced like the Skin Horse understand all about it.

'What is REAL?' asked the Rabbit one day, when they were lying side by side near the nursery fender, before Nana came to tidy the room. 'Does it mean having things that buzz inside you and a stick-out handle?'

'Real isn't how you are made,' said the Skin Horse. 'It's a thing that happens to you. When a child loves you for a long, long time, not just to play with, but REALLY loves you, then you become Real.'

'Does it hurt?' asked the Rabbit.

'Sometimes,' said the Skin Horse, for he was always truthful. 'When you are Real you don't mind being hurt.'

'Does it happen all at once, like being wound up,' he asked, 'or bit by bit?'

'It doesn't happen all at once,' said the Skin Horse. 'You become. It takes a long time. That's why it doesn't happen often to people who break easily, or have sharp edges, or who have to be carefully kept. Generally, by the time you are Real, most of your hair has been loved off, and your eyes drop out and you get loose in the joints and very shabby. But these things don't matter at all, because once you are Real you can't be ugly, except to people who don't understand.'

'I suppose you are Real?' said the Rabbit. And then he wished he had not said it, for he thought the Skin Horse might be sensitive. But the Skin Horse only smiled.

'The Boy's uncle made me Real,' he said. 'That was a great many years ago; but once you are Real you can't become unreal again. It lasts for always.'

The Velveteen Rabbit

The Rabbit sighed. He thought it would be a long time before this magic called Real happened to him. He longed to become Real, to know what it felt like; and yet the idea of growing shabby and losing his eyes and whiskers was rather sad. He wished that he could become it without these uncomfortable things happening to him.

There was a person called Nana who ruled the nursery. Sometimes she took no notice of the playthings lying about, and sometimes, for no reason whatever, she went swooping about like a great wind and hustled them away into cupboards. She called this 'tidying up', and the playthings all hated it, especially the tin ones. The Rabbit didn't mind it so much, for wherever he was thrown he came down softly.

One evening, when the Boy was going to bed, he couldn't find the china dog that always slept with him. Nana was in a hurry, and it was too much trouble to hunt for china dogs at bedtime, so she simply looked about her, and seeing that the toy-cupboard door stood open, she made a swoop.

'Here,' she said, 'take your old Bunny! He'll do to sleep with you!' And she dragged the Rabbit out by one ear, and put him into the Boy's arms.

That night, and for many nights after, the Velveteen Rabbit slept in the Boy's bed. At first he found it rather uncomfortable, for the Boy hugged him

very tight, and sometimes he rolled over
on him, and sometimes he pushed him
so far under the pillow that the Rabbit

could scarcely breathe. And he missed, too, those long moonlight hours in the nursery, when all the house was silent, and his talks with the Skin Horse. But very soon he grew to like it, for the Boy used to talk to him, and made nice tunnels for him under the bedclothes that he said were like the burrows the real rabbits lived in. And they had splendid games together, in whispers, when Nana had gone away to her supper and left the night-light burning on the mantelpiece. And when the Boy dropped off to sleep, the Rabbit would snuggle down close under his little warm chin and dream, with the Boy's hands clasped close round him all night long.

And so time went on, and the little

The Velveteen Rabbit

Rabbit was very happy – so happy that he never noticed how his beautiful velveteen fur was getting shabbier and shabbier, and his tail becoming unsewn, and all the pink was rubbed off his nose where the Boy had kissed him.

Spring came, and they had long days in the garden, for wherever the Boy went the Rabbit went too. He had rides in the wheelbarrow, and picnics on the grass,

and lovely fairy huts built for him under the raspberry canes behind the flower border. And once, when the Boy was called away suddenly to go out to tea, the Rabbit was left out on the lawn until long after dusk, and Nana had to come and look for him with the candle because the Boy couldn't go to sleep unless he was there. He was wet through with the dew and quite earthy from diving into the burrows the Boy had made for him in the flower bed, and Nana grumbled as she rubbed him off with a corner of her apron.

✷   ✷   ✷

That was a wonderful summer.

'You must have your old Bunny!' she said. 'Fancy all that fuss for a toy!'

The Boy sat up in bed and stretched out his hands.

'Give me my Bunny!' he said. 'You

mustn't say that. He isn't a toy. He's REAL!'

When the little Rabbit heard that he was happy, for he knew that what the Skin Horse had said was true at last. The nursery magic had happened to him, and he was a toy no longer. He was Real. The Boy himself had said it.

That night he was almost too happy to sleep, and so much love stirred in his little sawdust heart that it almost burst. And into his boot-button eyes, that had long ago lost their polish, there came a look of wisdom and beauty, so that even Nana noticed it next morning when she picked him up, and said, 'I declare if that old Bunny hasn't got quite a knowing expression!'

The Velveteen Rabbit

Near the house where they lived there was a wood, and in the long June evenings the Boy liked to go there after tea to play. He took the Velveteen Rabbit with him, and before he wandered off to pick flowers, or play at brigands among the trees, he always made the Rabbit a little nest somewhere among the bracken, where he would be quite

cosy, for he was a kind-hearted little boy and he liked Bunny to be comfortable. One evening, while the Rabbit was lying there alone, watching the ants that ran to and fro between his velvet paws in the grass, he saw two strange beings creep out of the tall bracken near him.

They were rabbits like himself, but quite furry and brand-new. They must

have been very well made, for their seams didn't show at all, and they changed shape in a queer way when they moved; one minute they were long and thin and the next minute fat and bunchy, instead of always staying the same like he did. Their feet padded softly on the ground, and they crept quite close to him, twitching their noses, while the Rabbit stared hard to see which side the clockwork stuck out, for he knew that people who jump generally have something to wind them up. But he couldn't see it. They were evidently a new kind of rabbit altogether.

They stared at him, and the little Rabbit stared back. And all the time their noses twitched.

'Why don't you get up and play with us?' one of them asked.

'I don't feel like it,' said the Rabbit, for he didn't want to explain that he had no clockwork.

'Ho!' said the furry rabbit. 'It's as easy as anything,' And he gave a big hop sideways and stood on his hind legs.

'I don't believe you can!' he said.

'I can!' said the little Rabbit. 'I can jump higher than anything!' He meant when the Boy threw him, but of course he didn't want to say so.

'Can you hop on your hind legs?' asked the furry rabbit.

That was a dreadful question, for the Velveteen Rabbit had no hind legs at all! The back of him was made all in one piece, like a pincushion. He sat still the bracken, and hoped that the other rabbits wouldn't notice.

'I don't want to!' he said again.

But the wild rabbits have very sharp eyes. And this one stretched out his neck and looked.

'He hasn't got any hind legs!' he called out. 'Fancy a rabbit without any hind legs!' And he began to laugh.

'I have!' cried the little Rabbit. 'I have got hind legs! I am sitting on them!'

'Then stretch them out and show me, like this!' said the wild rabbit. And he began to whirl round and dance, till the little Rabbit got quite dizzy.

'I don't like dancing,' he said. 'I'd rather sit still!'

But all the while he was longing to dance, for a funny new tickly feeling ran through him, and he felt he would give anything in the world to be able to jump about like these rabbits did.

The strange rabbit stopped dancing, and came quite close. He came so close this time that his long whiskers brushed the Velveteen Rabbit's ear, and then he wrinkled his nose suddenly and flattened his ears and jumped backwards.

'He doesn't smell right!' he exclaimed. 'He isn't a rabbit at all! He isn't real!'

'I am Real!' said the little Rabbit. 'I am Real! The Boy said so!' And he nearly began to cry.

Just then there was a sound of footsteps, and the Boy ran past near them, and with a stamp of feet and a flash of white tails the two strange rabbits disappeared.

'Come back and play with me!' called the little Rabbit. 'Oh, do come back! I know I am Real!'

But there was no answer, only the little ants ran to and fro, and the bracken swayed gently where the two strangers had passed. The Velveteen Rabbit was all alone.

'Oh, dear!' he thought. 'Why did they run away like that? Why couldn't they stop and talk to me?'

For a long time he lay very still, watching the bracken, and hoping that they would come back. But they never returned, and presently the sun sank lower and the little white moths fluttered out, and the Boy came and carried him home.

* * *

Weeks passed, and the little Rabbit grew very old and shabby, but the Boy loved him just as much. He loved him so hard that he loved all his whiskers off, and the pink lining to his ears turned grey, and his brown spots faded. He even began to lose his shape, and he scarcely looked like a rabbit any more, except to the Boy. To him he was always beautiful, and that was all that the little Rabbit cared about. He didn't mind how he looked to other people, because the nursery magic had made him Real, and when you are Real shabbiness doesn't matter.

And then, one day, the Boy was ill.

His face grew very flushed, and he talked in his sleep, and his little body was

so hot that it burned the
Rabbit when he held
him close. Strange
people came and
went in the
nursery, and a
light burned all
night and through it all the little
Velveteen Rabbit lay there, hidden from
sight under the bedclothes, and he never
stirred, for he was afraid that if they
found him someone might take him
away, and he knew that the Boy needed
him.

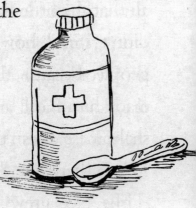

It was a long weary time, for the Boy
was too ill to play, and the little Rabbit
found it rather dull with nothing to do
all day long. But he snuggled down

patiently, and looked forward to the time when the Boy should be well again, and they would go out into the garden among the flowers and the butterflies and play splendid games in the raspberry thicket like they used to. All sorts of delightful things he planned, and while the Boy lay half asleep he crept up close to the pillow and whispered them in his ear. And

presently the fever turned, and the Boy got better. He was able to sit up in bed and look at picture-books, while the little Rabbit cuddled close at his side. And one day, they let him get up and dress.

It was a bright, sunny morning, and the windows stood wide open. They had carried the Boy out on to the balcony, wrapped in a shawl, and the little Rabbit lay tangled up among the bedclothes, thinking.

The Boy was going to the seaside tomorrow. Everything was arranged, and now it only remained to carry out the doctor's orders. They talked about it all, while the little Rabbit lay under the bedclothes, with just his head peeping out, and listened. The room was to be disinfected, and all the books and toys that the Boy had played with in bed must be burnt.

'Hurrah!' thought the little Rabbit. 'Tomorrow we shall go to the seaside!' For the Boy had often talked of the seaside, and he wanted very much to see the big waves coming in, and the tiny crabs, and the sandcastles.

Just then Nana caught sight of him.

'How about his old Bunny?' she asked.

'That?' said the doctor. 'Why, it's a mass of scarlet-fever germs! – Burn it at once. What? Nonsense! Get him a new one. He mustn't have that any more!'

And so the little Rabbit was put into a box with the old picture-books and a lot of rubbish, and carried out to the end of the garden behind the fowl-house. That was a fine place to make a bonfire, only the gardener was too busy just then to attend to it. He had the potatoes to dig and the green peas to gather, but next morning he promised to come quite early and burn the whole lot.

That night the Boy slept in a different bedroom, and he had a new bunny to sleep with him. It was a splendid bunny, all white plush with real-glass eyes, but the Boy was too excited to care very much about it. For tomorrow he was going to the seaside, and that in itself was such a wonderful thing that he could think of nothing else.

And while the Boy was asleep, dreaming of the seaside, the little Rabbit lay among the old picture-books in the corner behind the fowl-house, and he felt very lonely. The box had been left open, and so by wriggling a bit he was able to get his head through the top and look out. He was shivering a little, for he had

always been used to sleeping in a proper bed, and by this time his coat had worn so thin and threadbare from hugging that it was no longer any protection to him. Near by he could see the thicket of raspberry canes, growing tall and close like a tropical jungle, in whose shadow he had played with the Boy on bygone mornings. He thought of those long sunlit hours in the garden — how happy they were — and a great sadness came over him. He seemed to see them all pass before him, each more beautiful than the other: the fairy huts in the flower-bed; the quiet evenings in the wood when he lay in the bracken and the little ants ran over his paws; the wonderful day when he first knew that he was Real. He

thought of the Skin Horse, so wise and gentle, and all that he had told him. Of what use was it to be loved and lose one's beauty and become Real if it all ended like this? And a tear, a real tear, trickled down his little shabby velvet nose and fell to the ground.

And then a strange thing happened. For where the tear had fallen a flower grew out of the ground, a mysterious flower, not at all like any that grew in the garden. It had slender green leaves the colour of emeralds, and in the centre of the leaves a blossom like a golden cup. It was so beautiful that the little Rabbit forgot to cry and just lay there watching it. And presently the blossom opened, and out of it there stepped a fairy.

She was quite the loveliest fairy in the whole world. Her dress was of pearls and dewdrops, and there were flowers round her neck and in her hair, and her face was like the most perfect flower of all. And she came close to the little Rabbit and gathered him up in her arms and kissed

him on his velveteen nose that was all
damp from crying.

'Little Rabbit,' she said, 'don't you know who I am?'

The Rabbit looked up at her, and it seemed to him that he had seen her face before, but he couldn't think where.

'I am the nursery-magic Fairy,' she said. 'I take care of all the playthings that the children have loved. When they are old and worn out and the children don't need them any more, then I come and take them away with me and turn them into Real.'

'Wasn't I Real before?' asked the little Rabbit.

'You were Real to the Boy,' the Fairy said, 'because he loved you. Now you shall be Real to everyone.'

And she held the little Rabbit close in

her arms and flew with him into the wood.

It was light now, for the moon had risen. All the forest was beautiful, and the fronds of the bracken shone like frosted silver. In the open glade between the tree-trunks the wild rabbits danced with their shadows on the velvet grass, but when they saw the Fairy they all stopped dancing and stood round in a ring to stare at her.

'I've brought you a new playfellow,' the Fairy said. 'You must be very kind to him and teach him all he needs to know in Rabbit-land, for he is going to live with you for ever and ever!'

And she kissed the little Rabbit again and put him down on the grass.

'Run and play, little Rabbit!' she said.

But the little Rabbit sat quite still for a moment and never moved. For when he saw all the wild rabbits dancing around him he suddenly remembered about his hind legs, and he didn't want them to see that he was made all in one piece. He did not know that when the Fairy kissed him that last time she had changed him altogether. And he might have sat there a long time, too shy to move, if just then something hadn't tickled his nose, and before he thought what he was doing he lifted his hind toe to scratch it.

And he found that he actually had hind legs! Instead of dingy velveteen he had brown fur, soft and shiny, his ears twitched by themselves and his whiskers were so long that they brushed the grass. He gave one leap and the joy of using those hind legs was so great that he went springing about the turf on them, jumping sideways and whirling round as the others did, and he grew so excited that when at last he did stop to look for the Fairy she had gone.

He was a Real Rabbit at last, at home with the other rabbits.

* * *

Autumn passed and winter, and in the spring, when the days grew warm and sunny, the Boy went out to play in the wood behind the house. And while he was playing, two rabbits crept out from the bracken and peeped at him. One of them was brown all over, but the other had strange markings under his fur, as though long ago he had been spotted, and the spots still showed through. And about his little soft nose and his round black eyes there was something familiar, so that the Boy thought to himself: 'Why, he looks just like my old Bunny that was lost when I had scarlet fever!'

But he never knew that it really was his own Bunny, come back to look at the child who had first helped him to be Real.

THE THREE
BILLY GOATS
GRUFF

ONCE
UPON A TIME, IN A

faraway land, lived three Billy Goats all named Gruff. Their mother, you see, was not very creative and had a particular liking for the name, so by and by, they became known on the hillside as the Three Billy Goats Gruff.

As Billy Goats often do, they had eaten all of the lovely green grass and the

daisies that used to grow on the hillside and soon they became very hungry indeed.

One warm, sunny day the largest of the Gruff brothers declared that he was going to cross the bridge in search of grass, and if he was lucky, maybe some tasty oats.

'You can't possibly cross the Rickety Bridge, Big Brother Gruff, for Mother

The Three Billy Goats Gruff

said never to do so,' warned Little Gruff, who always followed the rules. 'But Mother is not here right now and I am so very hungry,' said Middle Gruff; 'if we are quick, we can be back on the hillside by the time she returns.'

Before any more discussion could be had, his two elder brothers darted towards the Rickety Bridge and the

youngest Billy Goat could do nothing but follow, for he had been told that when Mother was away, he was to listen to the eldest brother and do exactly as he said. Perhaps this was not such good advice after all?

When he arrived at the Rickety Bridge, the eldest brother said: 'Right, Little Gruff, you go first because you're the lightest and the bridge will certainly take your weight.'

Little Gruff knew that he did not have a choice so he began carefully to cross the bridge.

The Three Billy Goats Gruff

'Trip-trap, trip-trap,' went the bridge.

'WHO'S THAT tripping over my bridge?' roared the mean, hungry Troll, who lived underneath.

'Oh! It is only I, the tiniest Billy Goat Gruff; I am going to the other side to make myself fat,' he answered, in a small, trembling voice.

'No one dares cross my bridge! I am coming to gobble you up,' said the Troll.

'Oh, no! Please don't take me, I am far too little and would not make for a very filling meal,' said Little Gruff; 'why don't you wait for a bit until Middle Gruff comes along; he is much bigger than I.'

The little Billy Goat knew that the

middle brother was much too fast for the Troll to catch.

'Be off with you then,' said the Troll and Little Gruff happily obeyed and headed for the fresh, green grass on the other side.

A little while after, the second Billy Goat Gruff arrived, ready to cross the bridge.

'Trip-trap, trip-trap,' went the bridge.

'WHO'S THAT tripping over my bridge?' roared the Troll.

'Oh! It is I, the second Billy Goat Gruff, and I am going to the other side to make myself fat,' he replied, in not such a small voice.

'No one dares cross my bridge! I am coming to gobble you up,' said the Troll.

'Oh, no! Please don't take me, I am a fast-moving goat and I would be sure to upset your stomach. Why don't you wait for a bit until the biggest Billy Goat Gruff comes along for he is much bigger than I,' said the middle Billy Goat.

Middle Gruff knew that his elder brother was far too strong for the Troll to catch.

'Be off with you then,' said the Troll and Middle Gruff happily obeyed and headed for the fresh, green grass on the other side.

Very soon after, Big Billy Goat Gruff arrived, ready to cross the bridge.

'TRIP-TRAP, TRIP-TRAP,' went the bridge, for the eldest Billy Goat was so heavy that the bridge creaked and groaned underneath him.

'WHO'S THAT tripping over my bridge?' roared the Troll.

'IT IS I! THE BIG BILLY GOAT GRUFF,' he replied, in an equally thunderous voice.

'No one dares cross my bridge! I am coming to gobble you up,' roared the Troll.

'Well, come along! I have got two big horns, I am very strong and I am not scared of you,' shouted the eldest Billy Goat Gruff.

The Troll did not need asking twice. In no time he clambered on to the bridge.

'TRIP-TRAP, TRIP-TRAP,' went the bridge.

Big Gruff got himself into position; he lowered his horns and stamped his hooves as he prepared to charge. Then at the speed of light, he ran towards the mean, ugly Troll and hoisted him high into the air using just his mighty horns and tossed him over the Rickety Bridge.

The Troll landed in the river with an almighty SPLASH.

'You'll pay for this Big Gruff,' gurgled the Troll as he did his best to stay afloat.

As luck would have it, swimming under the bridge at that precise moment was a very hungry crocodile

who was in search of something big and tasty to eat.

Upon seeing the Troll splashing around in the water, the crocodile licked his scaly green lips and proceeded to gobble the nasty Troll up.

With that, the eldest Billy Goat Gruff happily crossed the bridge and headed for the fresh, green grass on the other side, where his brothers were eagerly munching away.

From that day forward, the Three Billy Goats Gruff were never hungry again and, with their Mother's permission, they were free to 'trip-trap' across the bridge any time they liked.

THE STORY
OF THE
THREE
LITTLE PIGS

ONCE
UPON A TIME THERE

was an old Sow with Three Little Pigs and when they were old enough she sent them out to seek their fortune.

The first Little Pig that went off met a Man with a bundle of straw, and said to him, 'Please, sir, may I have some straw to build myself a house?'

The Story of the Three Little Pigs

The Man gladly agreed, and the Little Pig got straight to work on building his straw home. Presently there came along a Wolf, and knocked at the door, and said, 'Little Pig, Little Pig, let me in.'

To which the Little Pig answered, 'No, no, by the hair of my chinny-chin-chin.'

'Then I'll huff, and I'll puff, and I'll blow your house down!' said the Wolf.

So he huffed, and he puffed, and he blew the house down, and gobbled up the Little Pig.

The Story of the Three Little Pigs

The second Little Pig met a Man with a bundle of wood, and said, 'Please, sir, may I have some wood to build myself a house?' The Man gladly agreed, and the Little Pig got straight to work on building his wooden home.

The Story of the Three Little Pigs

Then along came the Wolf and said, 'Little Pig, Little Pig, let me in.'

'No, no, by the hair of my chinny-chin-chin.'

'Then I'll puff, and I'll huff, and I'll blow your house down!' So he huffed, and he puffed, and he puffed, and he huffed, and at last he blew the house down, and gobbled up the second Little Pig.

The Story of the Three Little Pigs

The third
Little Pig met
a Man with a
load of bricks,
and said,
'Please, sir,
may I
have some
bricks to build myself a house?'

The Man gladly agreed, and the Little
Pig got straight to work on building his
brick home.

And the Wolf came once again and
said, 'Little Pig, Little Pig, let me in.'

'No, no, by the hair of my chinny-
chin-chin.'

'Then I'll huff, and I'll puff, and I'll
blow your house down.'

The Story of the Three Little Pigs

Well, he huffed, and he puffed, and he huffed, and he puffed, and he puffed, and he huffed, but he could *not* blow the house down. When he found that he could not, with all his huffing and puffing, blow the house down, he said, 'Little Pig, I know where there is a nice field of turnips.'

'Where?' said the Little Pig.

'Oh, in Mr Smith's field; and if you will be ready tomorrow morning, I will call for you, and we shall go together and get some for dinner.'

'Very well,' said the Little Pig, 'I will be ready. What time do you want to go?'

'Oh, at six o'clock.'

Well, the next morning, the Little Pig got up at five, and got the turnips and was home again before six. When the Wolf came he said, 'Little Pig, are you ready?'

'Ready!' said the little Pig. 'I have been and come back again, and have got a nice potful of turnips for dinner.'

The Wolf felt very angry at this, but not being an animal that gives up easily, he said, 'Little Pig, I know where there is a nice apple-tree.'

'Where?' said the Pig.

'Down at Merry Garden,' replied the Wolf; 'and if you will not deceive me, I will come for you at five o'clock tomorrow, and we will go together and get some apples.'

Well, the Little Pig woke up at four the next morning and went off to fetch some apples, hoping to get back before the Wolf came; but he had farther to go than he realised and had to climb the

tree, so he was delayed. Just as he was about to climb down, he saw the Wolf coming, which, as you may suppose, frightened him very much.

When the Wolf came up he said, 'Little Pig, once again you are here before me! Are they nice apples?'

'Yes, very,' said the little Pig; 'I will throw you one down.' And he threw it so far that while the Wolf was searching for it the Little Pig jumped down and ran home.

The next day the Wolf came again, and said to the Little Pig, 'Little Pig, there is a fair in the town this afternoon: will you go?'

'Oh, yes,' said the Little Pig, 'I will go; what time shall you be ready?'

'At three,' said the Wolf.

So the Little Pig went off before the time, as usual, and got to the fair, and bought himself a butter churn. Just as he was on his way home with it, he saw the Wolf coming towards him. The Little Pig did not know what to do, so he got inside the churn to hide, and in doing so, he knocked it down. The churn began to roll down the hill, faster and faster, with the Little Pig inside, and when the Wolf saw it he got such a fright that he ran home without going to the fair.

Very soon after, he went to the Little Pig's house to tell him how frightened he had been by a great round thing that came rolling down the hill towards him.

The Little Pig, feeling triumphant, said, 'Hah! I frightened you, did I? I had been to the fair and bought a butter churn, and when I saw you coming, I got into it, and it rolled down the hill.'

At that, the Wolf was very angry indeed, and declared that he *would* eat up the Little Pig, and that he would

get down the chimney after him if he had to.

When the Little Pig saw what the Wolf was about to do, he filled a pot full of water and placed it over the stove which had a blazing fire burning within it. Just as the Wolf was coming down, the Little Pig took the cover off of the pot, and in fell the Wolf.

The Little Pig quickly replaced the cover and, not being a fussy creature, he ate the Big Bad Wolf for dinner and lived happily ever after inside his brick house.

THE
FROG
PRINCE

ONE
FINE EVENING
A YOUNG PRINCESS

put on her bonnet and clogs, and went out to take a walk in the woods. After a while she came to a cool spring of water, so she sat down to rest for a while. She soon remembered that she had brought her golden ball with her, her favourite plaything, and she took it out and began tossing it up into the air and catching it again as it fell. After a time she threw it up so high that she failed to catch it and the ball bounded away and rolled along

the ground till at last it fell down into
the spring. The Princess looked into the
spring after her ball, but it was very deep,
so deep that she could not see the
bottom of it. Then she began to cry,
and said, 'Oh! If only I could get my ball
back again, I would give all my fine

clothes and jewels and everything that I have in the world.'

While she was speaking, a Frog popped its head out of the water, and said, 'Princess, why do you weep so bitterly?'

'I'm not sure you can help me, for you're just a Frog! My golden ball has fallen into the spring.'

The Frog replied, 'I want not your pearls, your jewels, nor your fine clothes; but if you will love me and let me live with you and eat off of your golden plate and sleep upon your bed, I will bring you your ball again.'

What nonsense, thought the Princess. He can't even get out of the spring to come and visit me, but, being a good swimmer, he might be able to get my ball

for me. I will just have to tell him that he can have whatever he wants.

So she said to the Frog: 'Well, if you bring me my ball, I will do whatever you ask.'

With that, the Frog put his head down and dived deep under the water. After a little while he came up again proudly, with the ball firmly in his mouth, and tossed it up on to the edge of the spring. As soon as the young Princess saw her ball, she ran to pick it up, and she was so overjoyed to have it in her little hands again that she never even thought of thanking the Frog. Instead, she hugged her ball tight and ran all the way home with it as fast as she could.

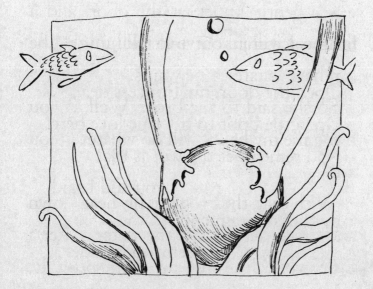

The Frog called after her: 'Come back, Princess, and take me with you, just like you promised.' But she did not stop to hear a single word.

The next day, just as the Princess sat down to have her dinner, she heard a strange noise — tap-tap-plash-plash — as if something was coming down the marble staircase. Soon afterwards there was a gentle knock at the door, and a little voice cried out and said:

Open the door, my Princess dear,
Open the door to thy true love here!
And remember the words that
                    you and I said
By the fountain cool, in the
                    greenwood shade.

The Princess jumped up and ran to the door and opened it, and there she saw the Frog, whom she had completely forgotten. At the sight of him, she felt quite sick; she slammed the door in his face and ran back to her seat. The King, her father, seeing that something had frightened her, asked her what was the matter.

'There is a nasty Frog at the door,' said she. 'Yesterday, he fetched my ball for me out of the spring and as a reward I told him that he could live here with me, thinking that he would never be able to get out of the spring; but there he is at the door, and he wants to come in.'

While she was speaking the Frog knocked on the door again, and said:

The Frog Prince

Open the door, my Princess dear,
Open the door to thy true love here!
And remember the words that
                              you and I said
By the fountain cool, in the
                      greenwood shade.

Then the King said to the young Princess: 'As you have given your word, you must keep it. Go and let him in.'

She did as her father said and let the Frog in. He quickly hopped into the room and came right up close to the table where the Princess sat.

'Please lift me on to a chair,' he said to the Princess, 'and let me sit next to you.'

As soon as she had done this, the Frog said: 'Put your plate nearer to me so that I may eat out of it too.'

This she did, and when he had eaten as much as he could, he said: 'I am very tired now; carry me upstairs, and put me into your bed, please.'

And the Princess, although she did not want to, took him up in her hand, and put him upon the pillow of her own bed, where he slept all night long. As soon as

it was light outside he jumped up, hopped downstairs and went out of the house.

Thank heavens, thought the Princess, at last he has gone, and I shall be troubled with him no more.

But she was mistaken. When night came around again she heard the same tapping at the door and she heard a familiar voice that said:

Open the door, my Princess dear,
Open the door to thy true love here!
And remember the words that
                    you and I said
By the fountain cool, in the
                    greenwood shade.

The Princess opened the door and the Frog came in, and, once again, slept upon her pillow until the morning broke. And the third night, he did the same. But when the Princess awoke on the third morning she was astonished to see not a slimy Frog in her bed but a handsome

Prince who had the most beautiful eyes that she had ever seen.

He explained that he had been enchanted by a spiteful Fairy who had cruelly turned him into a Frog and the only way to break the curse was to convince a beautiful Princess to let him eat from her plate and sleep upon her bed for three nights.

'You,' said the Prince, 'have broken the dreadful charm, and now I have nothing to wish for but that you should come with me to my father's kingdom, where I will marry you and love you for as long as you live.'

The young Princess, as you can imagine, took no time at all to say yes to all of this, and as they spoke

The Frog Prince

a splendid coach drove up, pulled by eight beautiful white horses, decked with plumes of silver feathers and golden harnesses, in preparation to whisk the happy couple away.

The Frog Prince

They bid farewell to the King and all the Princess's family and friends and got into the coach, which then set out towards the Prince's kingdom, where they lived happily ever after.

THE TALE OF
THE
CITY MOUSE
AND THE
COUNTRY
MOUSE

ONCE
UPON A TIME,
A LITTLE MOUSE

who lived in the country invited his friend, a little mouse from the city, to visit him. When the little City Mouse arrived he was quite surprised to discover that his friend lived in a rather shabby house. The Country Mouse, aware that his friend would be hungry after his long journey, had prepared the best dinner that he could. Being from the city, where food of every kind was available in abundance, the little City Mouse was quite surprised to find that the only food on offer was some old barley and grain.

'Really,' he said, 'you do not live well at all; you should see how I live! I have all sorts of fine things to eat every day. You must come and visit me and see how nice it is to live in the city.'

The little Country Mouse, who was quite fed up with stale grain for dinner,

was glad to oblige, and after a while he went to the city to visit his friend.

The very first place that the City Mouse took the Country Mouse to see was the inside of the larder of the house where he lived. There, on the lowest shelf, behind some jam jars, stood a big paper bag of brown sugar. The little City Mouse gnawed a hole in the bag and invited his friend to nibble for himself.

The two little
mice nibbled
and nibbled,
and the
Country Mouse
thought he had
never tasted
anything so
delicious in all
of his life. He
was just
thinking how

lucky the City Mouse was, when
suddenly the door opened with a bang
and in came the Cook to get some flour.

'Run!' squeaked the City Mouse. And
they ran as fast as they could to the little
hole by which they had come in. The

The Tale of the Two Mice

little Country Mouse was shaking all over, but the little City Mouse said, 'That is nothing; she will soon go away and then we can go back for more.'

After the Cook had gone away and shut the door they crept back to the larder, and this time the City Mouse had something new to show: he took the little Country Mouse to the corner of the top shelf, where a big jar of dried figs stood half open. After much tugging and pulling they got a large dried fig out of the jar and began to nibble away at it.

This was even better than the brown sugar. The little Country Mouse liked the taste so much that he could hardly nibble fast enough. But all at once, in the middle of their eating, there came a scratching at the door and a sharp, loud MIAOW!

'What is that?' said the Country Mouse, spurting fig juice everywhere. The City Mouse just whispered,

'Shhh!' and ran as fast as he could back to the hole.

The Country Mouse followed, you may be sure, as fast as he could. As soon as they were out of danger the City Mouse said, 'That was the old Cat; she is the best mouse hunter in town – if she so much as catches a glimpse of you, you are done for.'

'This is awful,' said the little Country Mouse; 'let us not go back to the larder ever again.'

'No,' agreed the City Mouse, 'I will take you to the cellar; there is something special in there.'

So the City Mouse guided his little friend down the cellar stairs and into a big cupboard where there were many shelves. On the shelves were jars of butter and cheeses in bags. Overhead hung bunches of sausages, and there were spicy apples in barrels. It all smelled so good that it went to the little Country Mouse's head. He ran along the shelf and nibbled at a lump of cheese here and a bit of butter there until he saw an especially rich, very delicious-smelling, piece of cheese on a queer little stand in a corner. He was just on the point of putting his teeth into the cheese when the City Mouse saw him.

'Stop, stop!' cried the City Mouse. 'That is a trap!'

The little Country Mouse stopped just as his front teeth were about to make contact with the cheese and said, 'What is a trap?'

'That thing is a trap,' said the little City Mouse. 'The minute you touch the cheese with your teeth something comes down on your head hard, and you're done for.'

The little Country Mouse looked at

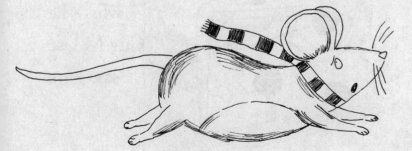

the trap, and he looked at the cheese, and he looked at the little City Mouse. 'If you'll excuse me,' he said, 'I think I will go home. I'd rather have stale barley and grain to eat and eat it in peace and

comfort than have brown sugar and dried figs and cheese – and be frightened to death all the time!'

So the little Country Mouse went back to his home, and there he stayed all the rest of his long and untroubled life, dining modestly maybe on only simple things but, most importantly, he was content and safe.

THE END